TRISTAR PICTURES PRESENTS A RICH-CREST ANIMATION PRODUCTION
A LIN OLIVER PRODUCTION A RICHARD RICH TERRY L. NOSS FILM "THE TRUMPET OF THE SWAN"
JASON ALEXANDER MARY STEENBURGEN REESE WITHERSPOON SETH GREEN
WITH CAROL BURNETT AND JOE MANTEGNA MUSIC BY MARCUS MILLER
CO-PRODUCER THOMAS J. TOBIN EXECUTIVE PRODUCER SELDON O. YOUNG PRODUCED BY LIN OLIVER
BASED ON THE BOOK BY E.B. WHITE SCREENPLAY BY JUDY ROTHMAN ROFÉ
DIRECTED BY RICHARD RICH TERRY L. NOSS

TRI STAR

© 2000 Tiny Tot Productions, Inc. All Rights Reserved.
© 2001 Tristar Pictures, Inc. All Rights Reserved.

The Trumpet Of the Swan

LOUIE GOES TO SCHOOL

Adaptation by Carol Pugliano-Martin
Based on the screenplay by Judy Rothman-Rofé
From the classic book by E. B. White

HarperFestival®
A Division of HarperCollins*Publishers*

One spring a baby swan was born.

His name was Louie.

Louie was different.

He could not speak.

Louie loved his family,
and they loved him.

But his parents worried about
their silent son.

When Louie saw a boy at the pond,
he thought of a way to say hello.

This boy, whose name was Sam,
liked animals very much.
Louie and Sam became good friends.

As Louie grew up,

he didn't like being different.

He wanted to be like the other swans.

He wanted to speak.

One day, Louie had an idea.
He would learn to read and write.
Then it wouldn't matter
that he didn't have a voice!
Louie decided to find Sam.
Sam would help him.

Back in Montana,
Sam was thinking about his
summer vacation at the pond.
He missed the little swan
who had untied his shoelace.

When Louie found Sam,
he said hello by untying Sam's shoelace.
Sam knew right away that it was Louie!
Now Louie had to make Sam understand
that he wanted to read and write.
How could he do it?

Louie pretended to write in the dirt.
Sam looked confused.
"What are you doing, Louie?"
Sam asked.

Louie grabbed Sam's book.

He turned the pages with his bill.

Suddenly Sam had an idea.

"You want to learn

to read and write!" said Sam.

Louie had made Sam understand!

The next morning,
Sam took Louie to school.
His first-grade teacher had taught
Sam to read and write.
Maybe she could teach Louie, too.

At Sam's old classroom,
Mrs. Hammerbotham smiled and said,
"Hello, Sam! Did you bring in your
pet for show-and-tell?"

17

"No, Mrs. Hammerbotham," said Sam.
"This is Louie. He wants to learn
to read and write."
Louie was scared.
He had never seen so many children!

Mrs. Hammerbotham was curious.
She wondered if she could teach
a swan to read and write.
Her class was curious, too.
They had never had a swan
as a classmate before.

First Louie tried to read.
It wasn't easy.

Then Louie tried to write.

It was hard for Louie to hold a pencil.

Mrs. Hammerbotham had an idea.
"Let's try writing with chalk, Louie,"
she said.

The chalkboard looked very big to Louie,
and the chalk looked very small.

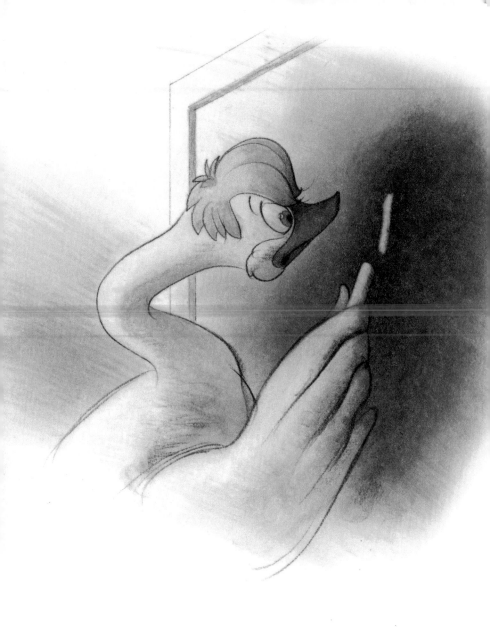

Louie kept trying until
he could hold a piece of chalk.

Louie tried very hard.

Soon he could write his own name!

The first-graders were very happy.
"Hooray for Louie!" they said.

Once Louie got started,
he didn't want to stop.
Louie loved writing!
He learned many new words.

Mrs. Hammerbotham was very
proud of Louie.

"Good job, Louie!" she said.

Now Louie didn't have to be sad
because he couldn't speak.
He had learned how to make
people understand.
It was time for Louie to go home.
He missed his family.

As they said good-bye,
Sam gave Louie a slate to wear
around his neck, and a bag full of chalk.
"Now you can write wherever you
are," said Sam.

Louie was sad to leave,
but he knew he would see
his good friend again soon.

As Louie flew home,
he felt proud of himself.
He had a voice at last!